It Is Friday

The Sound of FR

ROUND LAKE AREA
LIBRARY
906 HART ROAD
ROUND LAKE, IL 60073
(847) 546-7060

By Cynthia Amoroso and Bob Noyed

2

Friday is a fun day.

I never frown on Friday.

5

6

On Friday,
I run home
from school.

On Friday, I play with my friend.

9

10

On Friday,
I eat french fries.

On Friday,
I catch a frog.

13

14

On Friday,
I buy fresh fruit.

On Friday,
I sit on my
front porch.

17

18

On Friday, I get a gift from Aunt Fran.

Friday is the best day of the week.

Monday
Tuesday
Wednesday
Thursday
Friday
Saturday
Sunday

Word List:

Fran   frog
french fries   from
fresh   front
Friday   frown
friend   fruit

Note to Parents and Educators

The books in this series are based on current research, which supports the idea that our brains are pattern-detectors rather than rules-appliers. This means children learn to read easier when they are taught the familiar spelling patterns found in English. As children encounter more complex words, they have greater success in figuring out these words by using the spelling patterns.

Throughout the series, the texts allow the reader to practice and apply knowledge of the sounds in natural language. The books introduce sounds using familiar onsets and *rimes*, or spelling patterns, for reinforcement.

For example, the word *cat* might be used to present the short "a" sound, with the letter *c* being the onset and "_at" being the rime. This approach provides practice and reinforcement of the short "a" sound, as there are many familiar words made with the "_at" rime.

The stories and accompanying photographs in this series are based on time-honored concepts in children's literature: well-written, engaging texts and colorful, high-quality photographs combine to produce books that children want to read again and again.

Dr. Peg Ballard
Minnesota State University, Mankato

The Child's World®
childsworld.com

Published by The Child's World®
1980 Lookout Drive • Mankato, MN 56003-1705
800-599-READ • www.childsworld.com

PHOTO CREDITS
© acceptphoto/Shutterstock.com: 14; Bloomicon/Shutterstock.com: 21 (hand); Chantapa/Shutterstock.com: cover, 2; Franck Boston/Shutterstock.com: 21 (letters); In Green/Shutterstock.com: 5; karamysh/Shutterstock.com: 17; Kingarion/Shutterstock.com: 13; Nanette Grebe/Shutterstock.com: 9; Shutterstock.com: 18; Tatyana Vyc/Shutterstock.com: 6; Tobik/Shutterstock.com: 10

Copyright © 2018 by The Child's World®
All rights reserved. No part of this book may be reproduced or utilized in any form or by any means without written permission from the publisher.

ISBN 9781503819368
LCCN 2016960521

Printed in the United States of America
PA02337

ABOUT THE AUTHORS

Cynthia Amoroso holds undergraduate degrees in English and elementary education, and graduate degrees in curriculum and instruction as well as educational administration. She is currently an assistant superintendent in a suburban metropolitan school district. Cynthia's past roles include teacher, assistant principal, district reading coordinator, director of curriculum and instruction, and curriculum consultant. She has extensive experience in reading, literacy, curriculum development, professional development, and continuous improvement processes.

Bob Noyed started his career as a newspaper reporter and freelance writer. Since then, he has worked in school communications and public relations at the state and national levels. He continues to write for both children and adult audiences. Bob lives in Woodbury, Minnesota.